CALL ME
DISTURBING

_Live your
life to the moon and
back.
-FinnMott

By

Finn Mott

-A midnight light of hope buried
deep in the darkness of truth.

-A Declaration of Blooming Beginnings

-Dedicated to Dripping Paint

✯　　✯　　✯

Human howls at night, painted rocks scattered, lying just beneath sight, you remain prepared to shatter,

I try to live the lie the world said was okay but I can't help but sigh when my mind relays the non-existent graduation that was supposed to be mine.

Wandering through blinding darkness, a voice crackles under the strong steel tread of your leather boot.

Sparks of compassion and courage ignite off the quickening flame of COVID 19.

Fear becomes reality, laughs turn to sorrow.

The world turns grey.

Yet every gallon of grey paint has a drop of silver lining.

HERE IS MINE...

Paint your story-

“It may be stormy now but it will not rain forever”

✡ ✡ ✡

“A true friend sees the pain in your eyes while everybody else believes your smile”

✡ ✡ ✡

“We are all just a little bit f***** up”

✡ ✡ ✡

“There is a crack in everything. That is how the light gets in”

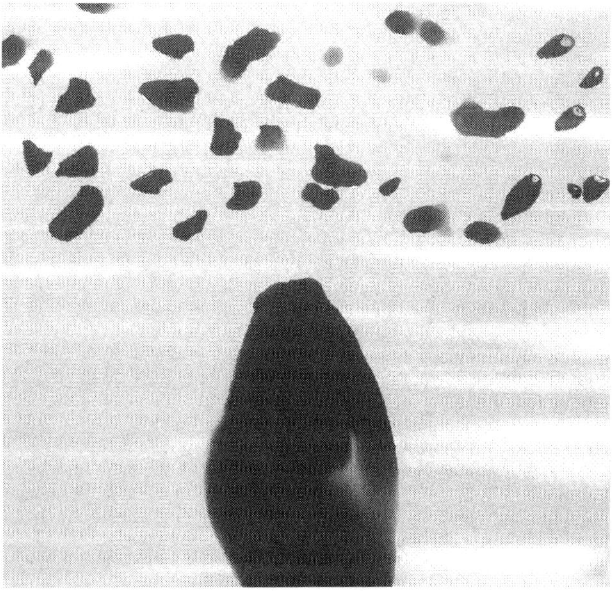

CONTENTS

Part III: Lump of Clay

Part IV: Legally to Be

Part VI: Sterilize Me

Acknowledgements

Thank you to all of the people from my hometown who have supported me through every adversity.

Thank you to all of my extended family.

Thank you to my Mom, my Step-Dad, and my Dad for supporting me and raising me. Thank you for inspiring a boy with big ambitions and even bigger dreams.

Thank you to all of my friends who have been there for me through thick and thin.

Thank you to Margaux Stavney for being one of the first to read my poetry and for being a damn cool person.

Thank you to Parker Labine for being an original and a person who never lets me down.

Thank you to my preschool teacher Anne Helene for giving me the love and excitement I needed to publish my work.

Thank you to all of my teachers for allowing me to ask many questions, for being there for me when I get overwhelmed, and for most importantly believing in me even when I did not.

Specifically, thank you to Mr. Knight for showing me the power of a war story, to Ms. Shapiro for helping me become passionate about sharing others' stories, to Mr. Tibboel for just being himself, to Mrs. Marsh for teaching me how to factor and how to focus on the learning instead of the grade, and to Mrs. Plain who taught me how to "reab".

Thank you to Mrs. Grilli for letting me cry in her office every other day, and to all of my counselors that got me through some deep shit.

Thank you to my lead Oncologist, Dr. Jean Levy, to my Endocrinologist, Dr. Megan Kelsey, to my neurologist, to my opthamologist, and all of the other doctors, departments, and nurses that saved my life.

Thank you to Rachel from Child Life and Erin from Oncology for being amazing nurses and down to Earth people.

Thank you to RoundUp River Ranch for inspiring me to keep fighting and to all of the campers and counselors I have met.

Thank you to my dogs who never fail to make me laugh and love me for who I unapologetically am.

Thank you to all of the people I have met who have helped shape who I am and to all of the tremendous opportunities that I have been blessed to have.

Thank you to my heros: Sean Swarner, Rupi Kuar, Tim O'Brien, Gerry Lopez, and Harry Potter.

Thank you to the coffee shops that have kept me grounded and sane and to the music that has given me permission to feel.

I have so many thanks to give to so many people. I am grateful for all of you, even if I do not know you (if you are reading this then I am thankful for you).

Thank you for being yourself because that is what matters most! Never change to be what somebody else thinks you should be.

Thank you to the two brain tumors and the spinal fluid that lived in my body and made me not okay because now, finally, I can be okay.

Author's Note

First of all, thank you so much for choosing to read my work. It truly means the world to me.

Secondly, I would like to provide some context in which this collection exists. We are living in a time of pain, destruction, and uncertainty. The world and this country are not okay. Excuse my language but a lot of things are really fucked up. We need to collectively and individually realize and accept that we are not okay. Only when we can feel and recognize this can we start healing.

Therefore, as you read the following words I pray for you to see beyond what your eyes cannot see. See beyond the pain and the hurt to the hope and the strength. This collection is not disturbing, it is real, and that is what this world needs. We all need to be real with what is going with society and within ourselves or we will never be able to move forward to a better future.

Again, thank you so much for choosing to read my work. I hope it can inspire you and give you a newfound sense of hope in whatever you may be dealing with.

PART I

GHOSTS

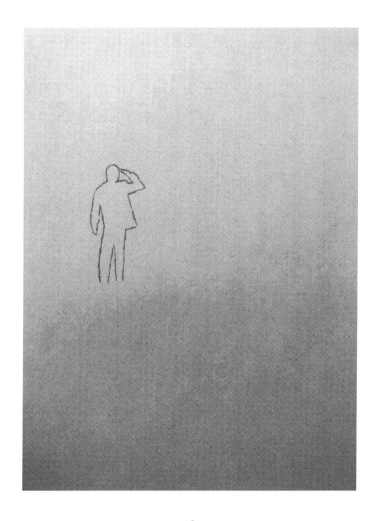

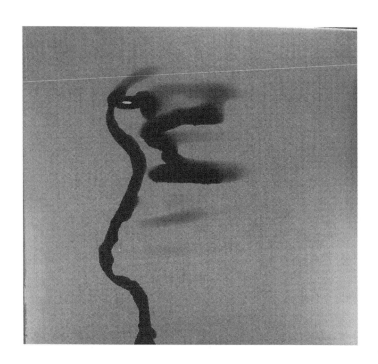

Remember Me

My town has held me in, shielding me from beyond vision, a place of ignorant sanity.

The one thing that let me forget, stripped from my grasp. In a world not my own, a false reality, superior not true.

Everything seems wrong but who am I to say so I dont.

What is simply a game of shame and guilt, I have seen it. I have felt it.

For some, there are only a few months left to breathe and smile. Why I wonder does the world not remember?

I was chosen to be different and yet, there is denial.

I feel like a target, you win if you hit the bullseye.

You win if you hit the bullseye.

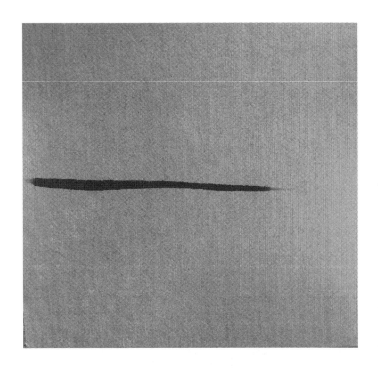

OKAY

Parked in the concrete of my youth,

my young self playing with a smile of innocence, jumping on the playground of my normality.

Up the wall, Over the bars, Down the slide.

And then, I trotted up toward myself and whispered, "It's okay."

"Wait!" I stammered but it was too late,

He was already gone.

FINN MOTT

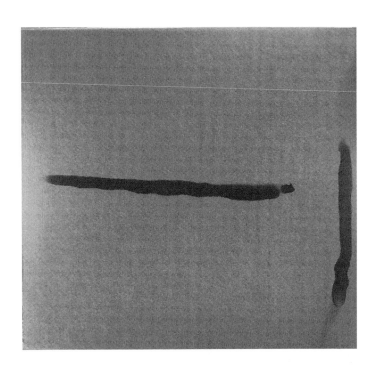

Black Cat

The world laid at our feet.

All that we have ever known and all the places we have ever been.

Our lives turn sometimes faster than the world spins.

The final year, sunrise to sunset.

We sat listening to the soundtracks of our youth, staring at the darkness that lies beyond, attempting to focus on why we are how we are?

The last sunset of our childhood ignorance falling off of the side of the world into the impending darkness that always wins the foot race.

My feet are bloody.

Suddenly out of the neighboring bushes leaps a black cat, its cries louder and louder as it scampers to our scarred knees.

-Our realities dictated by more than superstition.

MOSQUITO

My nails dig ever deeper irritating my already supple skin.

The unbearable itch finding its way through the labyrinth of my veins, cannonballing into my heart, and terrorizing my brain.

Day by day, I itch,

for the moment when everything is fine, or at least for the time I become blind.

I itch,

for my mother to be finally treated as she deserves.

I itch,

for the nights I can sleep absent of the immense regret I feel toward my unsatisfactory.

I itch,

for a time where the mosquito bites laced upon my withering body will no longer cry.

I itch

for the self capability to be confident even when I cannot say my name out loud.

I itch, with wonder,

is the world like my body; itching for a time free from the bloodsucking human beings we have come to be.

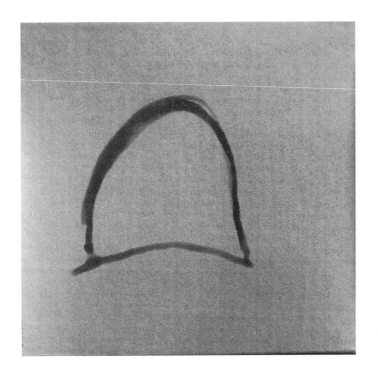

WE THE MURDERERS

I admire how grass always grows back, especially after it has been cut, killed, and conquered by the lifeless, improbable human expectations we all carry so tightly.

At peace the blades sit anxiously awaiting for their inevitable striking downfall implanted by our faulty attempt to one day be perfect.

CRACKED KNUCKLES

My knuckles stained with blood, cracked from the pressure to be sanitary.

My skin too tight, it might tear,

my burning palm clenched, dripping sweat.

The world has been cracked by COVID,

the palm of the world remains tightly tortured, dripping in alcohol.

-The road is long and it will sting but it is paved beckoning for us to follow.

DANDELION

Surrounded by blades, threatening to slice, a glimpse of hope.

Desperate for light to open its heart,
locked into a life unchosen, dominated by greed.

A weed it was born to be,
doesn't mean it can't bloom.

GUARDIANS

A leaf glistens in the newborn morning light strutting its green, perfect for all to see,

fitting unnoticed in the pack, dancing among their sacred guards who stand watch over the world's overarching shadows.

The forces of nature proved too powerful when the wind blows and sky huddles,

breaking from its home, falling free from its protection, left subject to the open world, droplet after droplet bury the life once lived until it cannot be found.

Only the essence remains.

In spirit it will live on, twirling in the wind, dancing in the rain, its duty to be the new guardian.

Our tears are like rain, full of downpour and destruction always leading to maturity and growth.

-As my skin warps I fear not of being alone
rather I fear having a lonely soul.

CROW'S CALL

I take a step outside, the air damp, clouds shielding the sun's vision,

streets lie empty calling for life.

For the first time in my life there is no sound,

except for one crow that calls out my name.

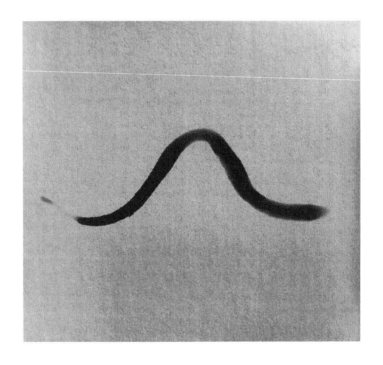

BLINKING LINE

You, it says,

"Use me and do not abuse me", it says.

I lie awake pondering how to create beauty out of a blank page?

How do I inspire a world overflowing with anguish?

And when I finally have the courage to put my pen to paper,

I don't understand.

HUMAN

In perfect tales the hero wins, morals perish evil.

In life, superpower is only a fatal dream,

light only thrives, buried deep within the heart of darkness.

Human vulnerability creates strength but nobody tells why are
there no stories of the human hero?

My bravery has leaked into the sewer,

only on paper can I try to possess tenacity.

In this city simplicity is unavailable, I wish to reverse the
modern fate.

DOUBLE VISION

An imaginary vision of a reality entirely my own does not allow my internal desperation to be visible to the stranger's eye.

Resolution is worthless unless we all decide to care more.

The broken lense encased over my eyes only exchangeable for total blindness,

or a

double vision reality,

I cannot see the world for what it is only for what I believe it could be,

let's make this vision a reality, together.

PART II

US

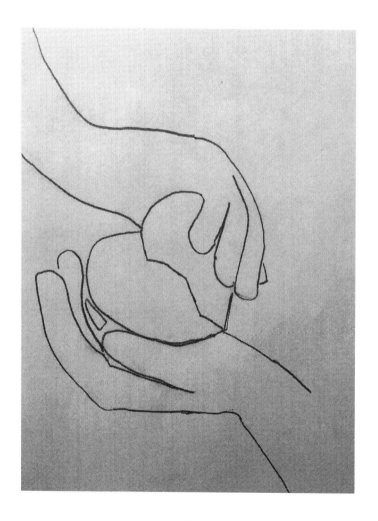

WALLS

When we talk my voice goes silent against my will, an invisible wall blocks normality,

so high, impossible to climb, too thick to penetrate.

I give up...

We fall into the same old mindless rhythm of victimizer and victim.

SOUL SLAYER

You place the problems of the world onto my frail shoulders,

when I cry for help you turn your back,

anger fills my lungs, I gasp for breath, my heart collapses.

Impossible for you to listen yet I pray.

Charred Ash

Singed to a crisp, colorless and black,

our intertwined core is brittle and fragile.

Your words are the gasoline awaiting to be lit by my eager hope
that kneels down for your demonic spirit to finally evolve into
something with a compassionate heart.

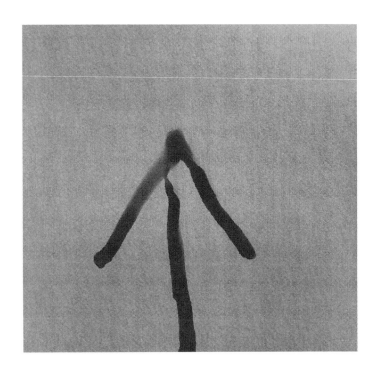

SELECTIVE FAVORITISM

A one way mirror of acknowledgment, a conversation of manipulation, validation for one and only one.

Can't you see every time you choose to ignore you hurt, you damage, you distance our hearts and our relationship.

I listen to the ways she is slowly hammered down into a deepening rut of deception,

the cold way I am never noticed for what I do,

but as soon as your biology enters praise is plentiful.

Tireless days and nights you refuse to look beyond, your lack of gratification can kill and has killed us.

I do not want to be dead,

please recognize my name and her sorrowful soul.

America is like Movie Night

The grandest time comes, when we all can sit together to let our minds slip from the treacherous reality,

and your thumbs twiddle and words twist around until you have chosen your pick,

the cover screen is full of blood and bullets, I squint my eyes and shake my head trying to send any signal,

but you look away, turn your head, and firmly say no whenever anybody else speaks.

This is not the movie night I dreamed of, this is your opportunity to be the dictator you have never failed to be, over and over your picks bulldoze over any say anybody else could have until it is just you and we are all lying dead on the floor.

What type of family is this?   IS IT?

Just like America you promise equal freedom of opportunity but never do you follow through with your hollow words in this one sided household.

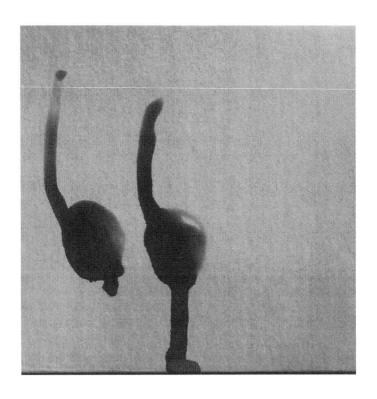

"That's What I am Saying"

The phrase itself ridicules the other and boasts the self,

every other line you employ the tool to make all else feel less than your notable ego.

I want to respond with, "No! That is not what you're saying! That is what you are manipulating!" but I can't because I don't want to hurt her anymore than I already have.

I am left with defeating silence because I am too afraid to say anything that will disrupt the tense peace.

I will not be here long so the problem of me will disappear soon, but every day I will worry about the true way you are treating her.

I believe you are good, I pray you will give her what she deserves.

UKULELE

Tighter and tighter you twist me, my screams become higher and higher until the human ear cannot hear me scream any longer.

Your grasp amplifies until my lifeline snaps with a loud crack, unfixable and useless I become.

Leave me alone...

If only you would listen to the elegant music I was born to play.

Tug of War

Exhausted from living my life as a tightening knot at the center of a never ending tug of war,

pulled by the two people who should love me most, my ends are fraying

-Only under unachievable conditions will I instill external calm.

Retie my weaknesses, burn my edges till they harden and turn black.

My greatest fault lies in the failure to maintain internal peace in a world of eternal conflict,

the most devastating world war rages on inside my wrongly compassionate heart.

BEND

My body is stiff and rigid,

point to a part of me, I'll tell you what's wrong.

I daydream when I could do anything, run faster than the wind, remain dry in the rain,

jump among the clouds.

But now I am stuck in a casket of my own design, 6 feet deep my beating heart lies.

My body does not bend, it will only snap.

Meri Go Around

Round and round our words spin,

expertly you twist my tongue molding it to fit your narcissistic desires.

Through the center of the Earth, I can dig until I will, at last, discover the true color of your black heart.

Never will I be able to read the devilish language off your lips,

Why do you say what you do not do?

I am dizzy, I am tired, I am no longer a child,

stop spinning me on this Merry Go Around.

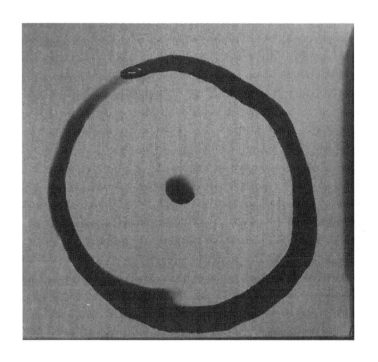

ACCOMMODATE ME

People say my brain works differently, I want to believe I am normal but something within me does not allow regularity to persist.

Contradicting forces constantly at work.

If I am special something is wrong, why does everybody struggle to be the same?

The world seems to drive around me as if I am the center of a roundabout,

never touched by the dirty treads but glared at by all, surrounded by grey concrete, I stick out brighter than I wish to be,

it would be more efficient if I was a straight line

-deconstruct me and repave.

PART III

LUMP OF CLAY

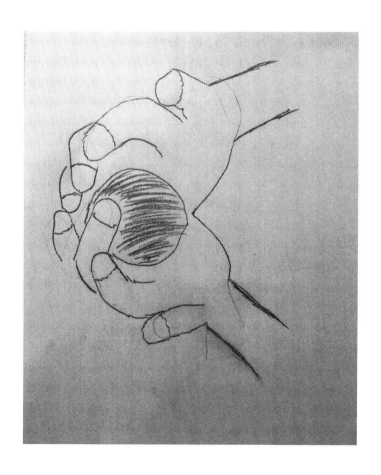

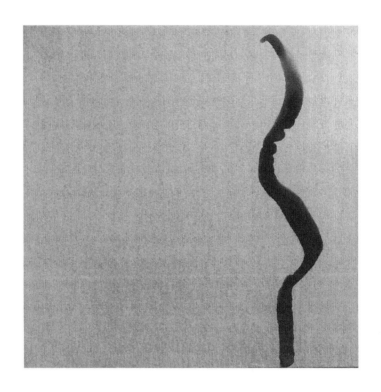

THE DEVIL'S REFLECTION

Adrenaline rushes when I step
on the plastic devil,

it shouts numbers at me.

With covered ears something scampers into my brain
and toxicity invades.

I want to smash, to starve, to cry, but I don't.
I can't...

My breath filled with furocity at the devil reflected by the evil
scale.

Chocolate

My teeth hurt when I eat chocolate,
I keep eating anyway.

CHERISH

I want to share, I dream to be rare.

Why do I even care? When it only is a tear.

I want to be more than rubbish, I dream to be published.

Who says when I am established? All I need is to be cherished.

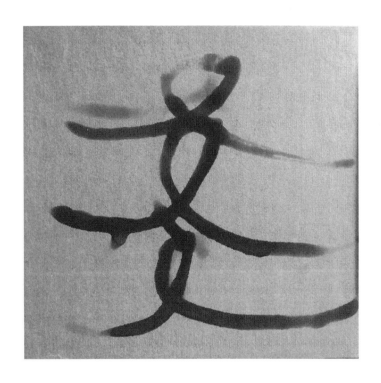

DRIFTING IN THE WIND

I am scared to touch the world I am supposed to explore,
instead I walk without gravity.

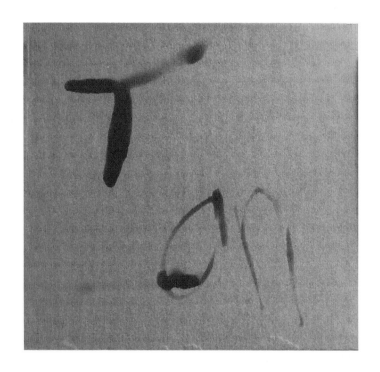

WHAT AM I?

I exist on a screen, to be a teen I am not.

I am my words, my words are me, we are each other.

Maybe to be read, or to be abandoned.

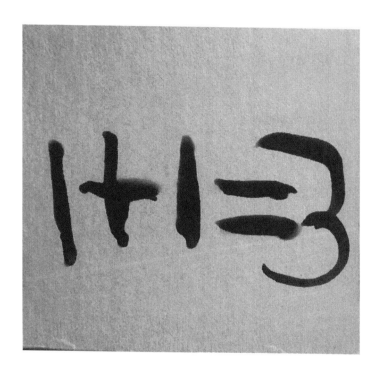

POETRY+PASSION=PURPOSE

I am an equation that can't be solved,

I have no solution.

I am a canyon with no river, dried from the wandering wind climbing up my walls.

I am a jack in the box unable to sing, twisted too tightly.

I am a blaring noise that blocks the sweet sound of a playing harp.

I am unknown to myself,

but you know me, you hear the voice that whispers within me.

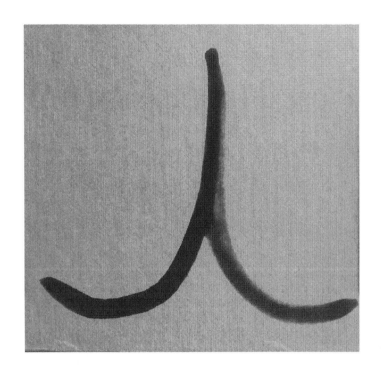

LIVING TO DIE

It is a shame that to be alive means knowing when you are dead. Some of me is lost, most of me is broken.

but this is my therapy, and if you can carry this on then I will never die.

BARREN

My most concerning thought is that my shaking hand will never do justice to my mindless and emotional self inflicted war.

If anything, I dream for you to let this be a beacon of light in a world of uncertain darkness.

PART IV

LEGALLY TO BE

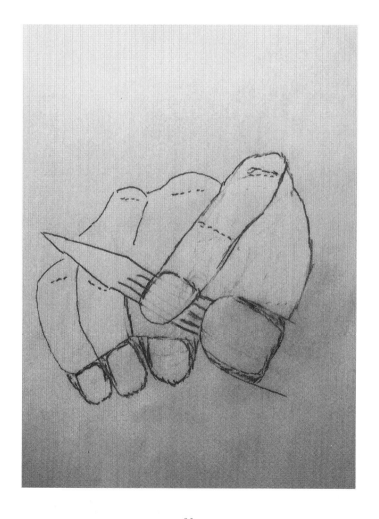

BLANK NAME

How to spell?

my lines never straight, so simple, so sweet yet, still unwritten,

I feel like my name is not my own.

Never available for purchase, too rare, too insignificant.

I wonder if life would be easier if I left my name blank.

Hi, my name is ____.

WHICH ONE?

Is mentality my reality?
Is reality my mentality?

I know I am mental but am I real?
I want to be real.

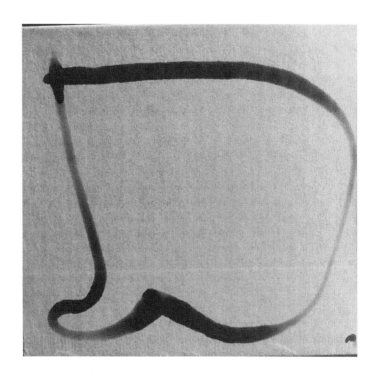

MINDFUL MINDLESSNESS

I cannot decide if I would rather be mindful or mindless.

Knowledge is a privilege and should never be abandoned or obstructed,

but it would be so easy, so simple, so sweet,

to be ignorant.

MY MASK

Demanded to cover our identities,

original voice ferociously filtered.

We conceal the smile, tears left to be displayed.

Little does the world know I have worn a mask for years.

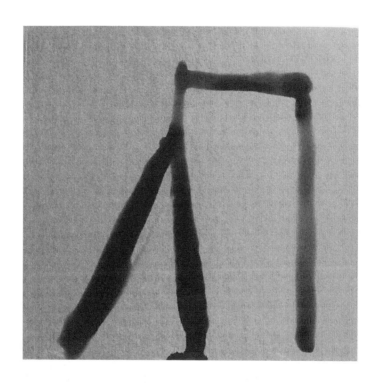

WE BOW OUR HEADS

Only you, my companion,

when we each lean on each other and breath deep together,

despite being a dog, you know more than any other friend knows about me.

Seeing me with the absence of fear to be seen and labeled.

My Dude, my dog, my companion for eternity.

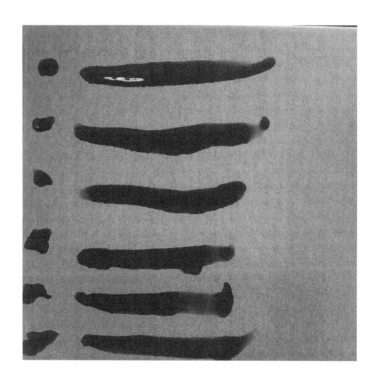

THE LIST

Double digits,

issues boil out, every surgery causes resurges.

"It will help you grow", they say,

"How?" I say.

My legs black and blue from my indestructible nemesis,

I strike myself with kryptonite, the burn never lifts.

My hatred is not justified by the exponential growth.

-to inspire we need to suffer.

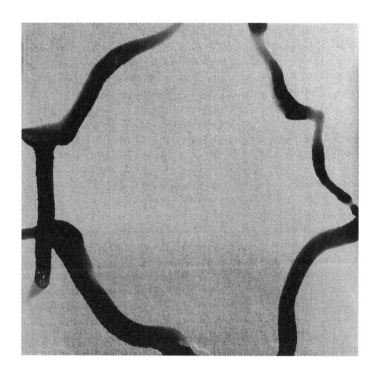

DISH WATER

Yellow, and raggedy an old sponge I treasure,
used for wiping up leftovers
not chosen.

I clean over and over with hope for a thank you,
rarely does one come.

-I feel like dirty dish water.

UNGRATEFUL CRITICISM

She does a million things you will never know about, she has that humble ability,

meanwhile the instant you do anything you demand respect and gratification.

And in the rare instance when she does tell, you do not say, "Thank you",

you say, "Well I don't like..., or I would have done…",

never do you appreciate it unless it is youself or your true son.

There is no recognition of others' pain or work, take all of the credit now and know that it is you who made this house fall apart.

I am not your son, but you are all the father I have and I do not want to be silenced any longer.

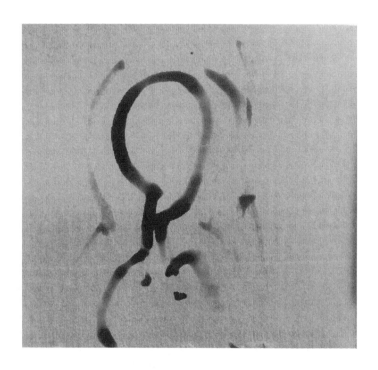

SILHOUETTE

My words do not count unless you choose not to hear but to listen.

The conscious effort to help, to supplement your melting presence,

only in your gain do you finally have solidity.

This house caged into a corrupt culture, a prison,

how long will it take to see that you are deleting the words of those around you?

There is no undo button.

We are nothing but a silhouette in your shadow. Please look past what your eyes refuse to see.

See me, see us, see this.

I could write a million pages but none of them would matter if you do not choose to read them.

DIRTY FINGERNAILS

"You look like a girl, Why don't you cut?"

I answer but my replies never suffice the sharp ridicule,

what if I told you I like the way dirt fills my inadequate underbelly?
I like the way the grime makes me feel alive,
I hate the way you chisel me apart, as if looking for a hidden
gem that must lie beneath the shameful surface, my skin
irritated and thin from your constant scratching,
I will always be a pile of dirt to you.

My nails are long to embrace the dead you have erupted,
my bed is wrinkled for the monster you have allowed to live
under,
my voice is absent because I cannot yell loud enough to
penetrate the wall I have been forced to construct.

I walk without you to step on the fatal pressures you press
upon my face suffocating my breath and dampening my spirit.

My body stays asleep for it is too afraid to expose its delicate
self.

My cuticles are bloody and broken but my fingers will never
be cut short
from your ruthless voice again.

TREMBLE

My hands shake to a silent rhythm, my veins bulge out of my skin.

I love it when my body trembles, it reminds me how alive I am,

-it is easy to forget we are breakable.

We are breakable...

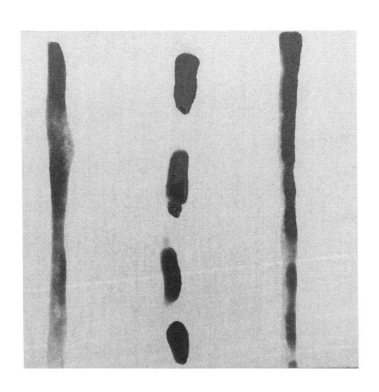

STAGNANT SECONDS

White never mixes with yellow,

for miles, infinitely we can travel letting time drift by waiting for change.

I drive at night following the humble torch ignited by the starving artist.

CRESCENT

Ticking away to the tune of our pulsing blood and beating hearts,

the timer of life awaits for our fatal decisions that either make us known or forgotten.

To short to understand, to long to appreciate,

each moment is a blessing disguised in material design.

-it is your responsibility to scratch beneath the crest and find the crescent that lies within.

LET ME

I see pictures of the perfect,
I wonder how, if, truth exists.

Over and over I tremble, I shake with indecency,
my body hurts, it cries for me to forgive, to accept,
"No," I say.

I perform never to the level I desire.

In the mirror my skin droops, acne dances, face remains
disfigured, scars stick out like knives.
I wish they could stab me.

The time is terribly perfect for the self but no matter how
excruciating I try it never works wonders,

-let me have something please.

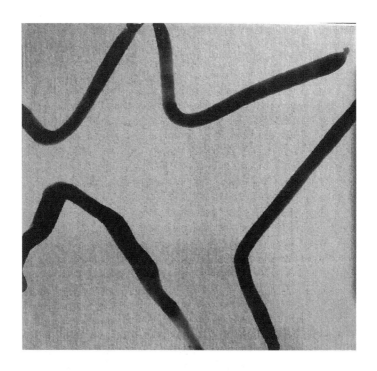

COULD IT BE?

You and me,

finally doing the thing called father and son, maybe,

could it be, you are making an effort beyond yourself,

could it be, you are validating the sour person your fiance is to me,

could it be, could it be, could it be,

you have realized my time as your child is gone,

and that I may, just maybe, am more important than your work.

It is not perfect, and it never will be, but it could be something more than the turmoil and isolation,

more than the fear and the disgust,

more than the distrust and ridicule,

more than the bullets and shields,

more than the hate,

-maybe...

it could be.

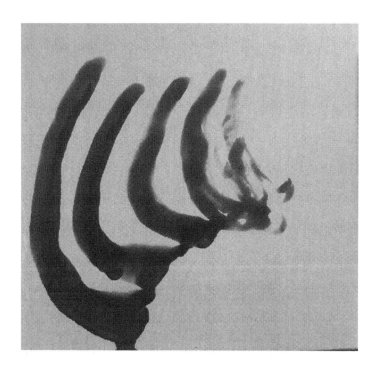

C WORDS

First Cancer now COVID.

This world, my world is dictated by the prison of illness.

Come find me, if you have the courage, I will be your greatest regret,

try and capture me, I dare you...

PART V

INFECTED

HOLES

My brain defined by the two holes that made me nothing more than a patient,

I try to cover up what will never be filled in.

I will always live broken, left never to be whole.

COVID is only a number added to the list.

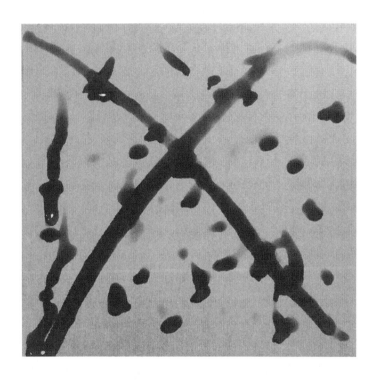

DOTS

My youth is illustrated by beautiful pictures created with nothing but lines and dots,

now, one moment does not predict the next.

Impossible to connect the future,

only backwards can we make sense.

-I wish I could still connect the dots.

P

Pain is power,

Power is potential,

Potential is purpose.

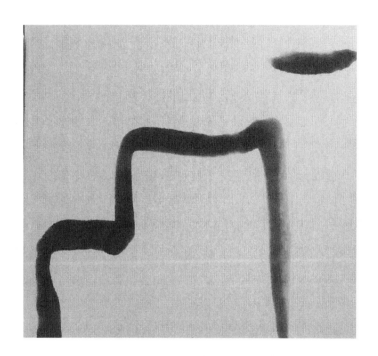

ALMOST 18

So close, adulthood haunts me,

I am not ready, I do not want to be ready.

Leaving everything I have ever known for a life undiscovered.

Barely able to handle COVID how will I survive let alone thrive?

DISCLOSURE

Cured I may be, poison lurks at my feet,

one wrong step and I will not be pure,

so sure I was, turned out to be lured to a fate untrue.

-my only tenure is literature.

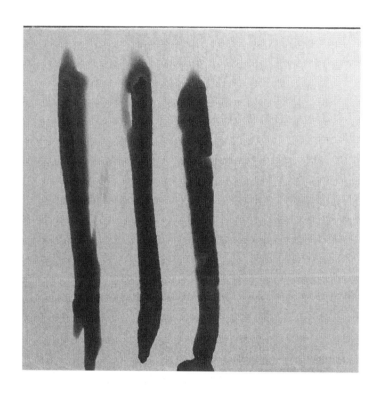

GUILTILY ILL

I am guilty,

for my fatality is my only liability.

A threshold of insanity persists under my sacred veins threatening to collapse.

An infamous sour sensation of a metal cylinder underneath my blank skin, morbidly excruciating.

Sick I am,

-I like it though.

BREAK THE UNBREAKABLE

I will never be the son you want me to be.

called, "selfish and disturbing".

Words misalign with your actions.

I can't keep placing false hope into what we could be and ignoring what we are,

an unbreakable circle, the least you can do is let me be free before you break me beyond repair.

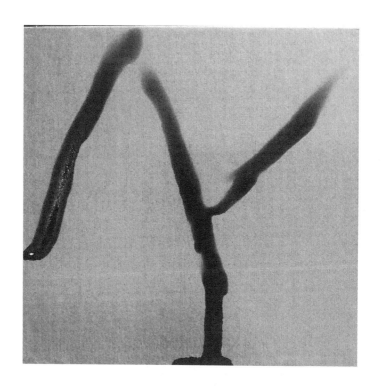

SOUR

In my car sipping sour sweet,

cold rain thudded, rushing water dribbled,

till I stopped to stare at the foggy distance blanketing the sloping hill

Minutes Hours Days,

when will life not be so sour?

KICK AND CHASE

I was running fast, my legs numb.

Life was kick and chase, constantly hoping to be an impossible ideal, brainwashed to follow an invisible door placed on an unpoppable bubble,

perfect seemed to exist.

I was wrong...

no matter how much I changed nobody wanted to see, nobody could see, nobody decided to see-

me

Until one day,

I cracked in half like a glowstick, unable to light, remaining grey,

my life turned to a drizzle, a hailstorm,

until no more tears could fall from my eyes, unable to blink.

Little by little my light was collected and rekindled,

the bubble joined together to finally see something past perfect,

they saw me, bald and weak, imperfect I was,

needle by needle we popped the bubble of perfect.

Suddenly aware of myself,

each stroke hurt ever more until my legs became weightless and my body tingled with numbness,

at last I surmounted the journey that has given me infinite agony.

My past and my present, only allow a reaction.

a descent it may be, the bottom beneath me, grounding me, fueling me.

The trail is straight, but it is destined to turn,

for whatever comes my way, I know I can climb any mountain,

-I will breathe at any elevation.

CALL ME DISTURBING

PARADISE ON EARTH

Materially it does not exist, nowhere and everywhere,

only in your mind can you travel the long journey,

through the cave of nightmares, into the forest of regret, skipping over proud waterful, and climbing confident peak,

eventually, you will arrive naked and afraid, ready for paradise to finally be real.

I am ready...

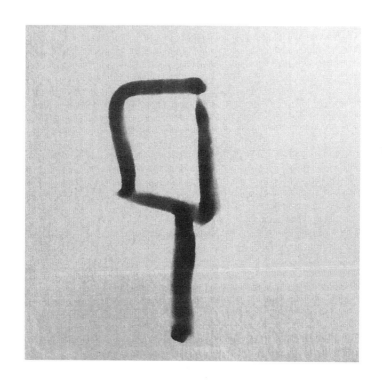

NO OVERNIGHT PARKING

If my trust were a parking lot,

there would be No Overnight Parking.

Time after time I open my heart to the warmth of the summer sun and the world never fails to pierce my faith with a frozen icicle.

I am ready for the cold to finally melt out of my poisonous blood.

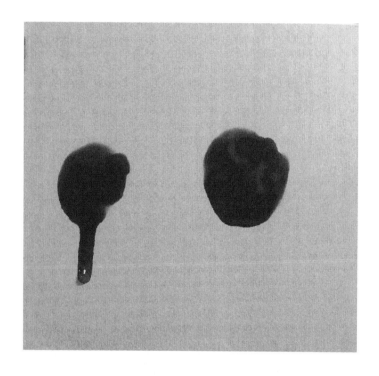

Four-Legged

The chilled breeze and I staring whole-heartedly at the world
I am left to paint, the only blank space I can write my legal
name is this,

my rhymeless words a comforter too heavy for me to lift
protecting my pale skin from the angry sun,

my savior lying with me, four legs and all, seeing the me
unknown and misunderstood,

together we listen to the chilled wind of my words.

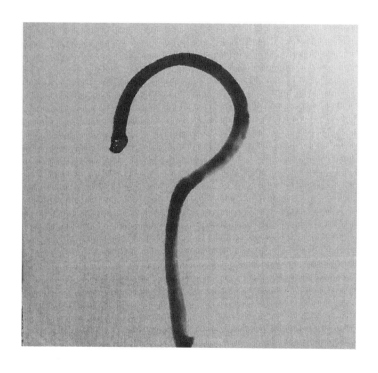

QUESTION MARK

I lie to feel better about the disturbing reality,
secretly my sorrow has another reality.

What is real? What is normal? What is this?

So many questions that will never be answered.

How can I continue?
except for through this.
Thank you...

PART VI

STERILIZE ME

FORGIVE ME

Forgive me for the sins I have committed,

forgive me for the cage I have built around myself and for letting the only key sink to the bottom of the deepest ocean,

forgive me for failing to be enough. forgive me for being the problem in your life. forgive me for me,

for the failing fight I have gripped so tightly,

for the crumpled piece of paper I have become,

and the wrinkled scars that permanently define me,

and for being scribbled upon with a black pen,

forgive me for the fate fictitiously designed for my becoming,

-forgive me and help me find me.

PLEASE ACCEPT AN APOLOGY

I am sorry for the sorrowful excuse I am of a man,

until I prove what I am, I will keep beating the sensitivity out of me, I will continue to stab my heart, yet every time I pierce my scarred skin and I bleed,

my superpower only swells ever more.

I am sorry,

I will never be cold blooded.

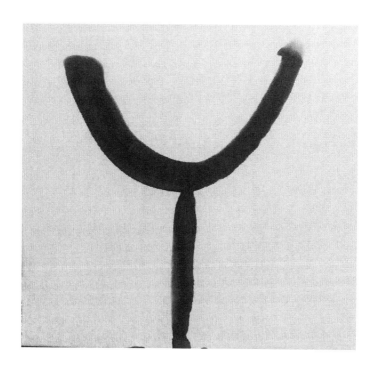

BRUISED NOT BROKEN

My legs are bruised from the needles that pierce my skin,
every night I question whether my pain will ever be recognized.

Forever I will do what I have to do to remain strong and have hope, knowing sometimes that I may become bruised and believing I will never be broken,

-I am, this, and this is perfect no matter what you say.

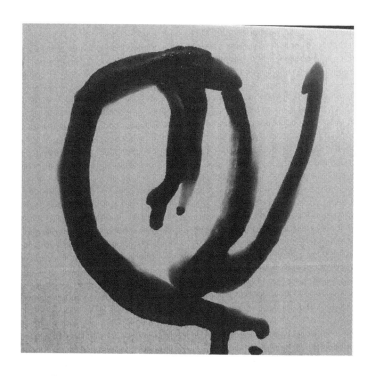

HEALED HANDS

Our grip on reality strained, our grip among each other enhanced behind bonding adversity.

Time may make our fingers slip but there will always be somebody there to catch our fall,

-my hands may have been wounded but they will never be worthless.

DEAR COVID 19,

I am only a voice of the billions,

I am only a boy fighting his own battle, and I may be damaged but I am not defeated.

You have taken, destroyed, and stomped on many things,

however, I promised myself, long ago, to never let my pain commandeer my life,

no matter how heartless your impact may be,

my spirit will only glow brighter and my love will only become more indestructible.

-my tears foster my passion to turn words into a tree of life.

Sincerely, me

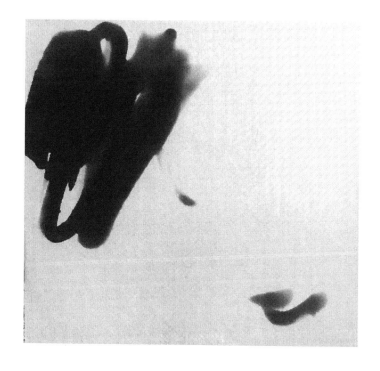

MODERN MEDICINE

With every step, the plastic box rattles in sync with my skipping heartbeat,

crucial for my survival I rely on the small pills I do not understand,

prescribed to a reality, saved from the coming darkness,

dependent on the Modern Medicine that killed and destroyed, saved and rebirthed.

-I am unable to decide what I have to do, only to react with a positive perspective.

SCAR TISSUE

Behind the golden pins that mark my excellence lies the 4 inch dotted line where the plastic implanted above my heart was stolen.

My jingling awards bouncing upon my graduation gown do not understand, are not able to see what my body truly looks like, how my determination artfully developed by the synchronizing needles of vain vulnerability.

-the scar tissue on my body dries my tears.

EXPENSIVE FATE

Lost in twirling confusion, we are muddled, looking to escape the tax called life.

Gaining what the other does not, this is how you survive, stammering over the softer voice, stepping on the broken,

brutality is the lifestyle.

Sometimes I forget,

if it is possible to live in anti tyranny?

Tell me, I do not know...

CLARITY

Perfectly still, water droplets,

they exist in a state of everlasting peace and ultimate content,

fearless to be what it was born to be, prepared to roar if need be.

With subtle transparency the feeling of cold running water with absolute clarity down my cracked palms.

If only my mind could be of such peace, but even in times of sanity the only clarity is confusion.

How can I close my dam? How do I shut the valve?

-I will never run dry for as long as I have you.

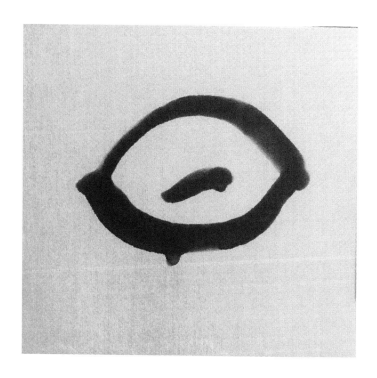

TOMORROW

For all of you who don't know tomorrow,

remember the voices that call out your name and bathe in love for your individuality is beyond precious.

Remember,

the bittersweet smell of fine brewed coffee and sip with genuinity staring into the beautiful blue eyes of your fantastical friends.

Remember,

the frustrating chirp of the twinkle birds singing whimsical songs that do not need to be understood.

Remember,

the person who grounds you and keeps you sane even when the world may be full of war,

feel the warm hug that comforts you through pain and sorrow and excites you in times of growth and celebration.

Remember,

you are beautifully imperfect no matter what others say, and nobody can ever take that away from you.

Remember,

your health is your heart, the more you suffer the more you feel,

your gratitude for yourself, and the little things is everything even when it may feel like nothing.

-you are everything.

UNIVERSAL TRUTH

Stories the only thing carried through time, the greatest power of the world,

above all are the morals and human heroes that attempt to explain how we should be living.

The beauty lies within interpretation,

a noble knight or

a vicious villain,

you choose…

I AM OKAY

My life will never be the same,

I will always have timid hands and scarred skin, my brain will remain hollow until I find the words to articulate what I feel I have lost.

Every moment and every day is beyond terrifying, I will cry, I will tremble,

I will laugh.

This magical release never fails to help me explain what I struggle to feel, to smile through my tears.

This makes me okay, please find yours.

Finale: Thank You

My definition will never be Cancer or COVID,

my evolution will always be writing.

Call me sick or sad,

call me by name or not,

Just please, do not "Call Me Disturbing" because I am much, much more,

and never again will I feel sorry for who I am.

My name is Finn, what is yours?